This Book Belongs to:

....

Consultant: Fiona Moss, RE Adviser at RE Today Services
Editor: Cathy Jones
Designer: Chris Fraser
Editorial Assistant: Tasha Percy
Design Manager: Anna Lubecka

Copyright © QEB Publishing, Inc. 2014

First published in the United States in 2014 by
QEB Publishing, Inc.
3 Wrigley, Suite A
Irvine, CA92618

www.qed-publishing.co.uk

A CIP record for this book is available
from the Library of Congress.

ISBN 978 1 60992 496 6

Printed in China

Jesus and his Disciples

Written by
Katherine Sully

QEB Publishing

Illustrated by
Simona Sanfilippo

When Jesus was a young man, he traveled from village to village teaching God's message.

Wherever he went, people came to hear the stories he told.

Soon, lots of people had heard about Jesus.
Whenever he arrived in a village, a crowd
quickly gathered to meet him.

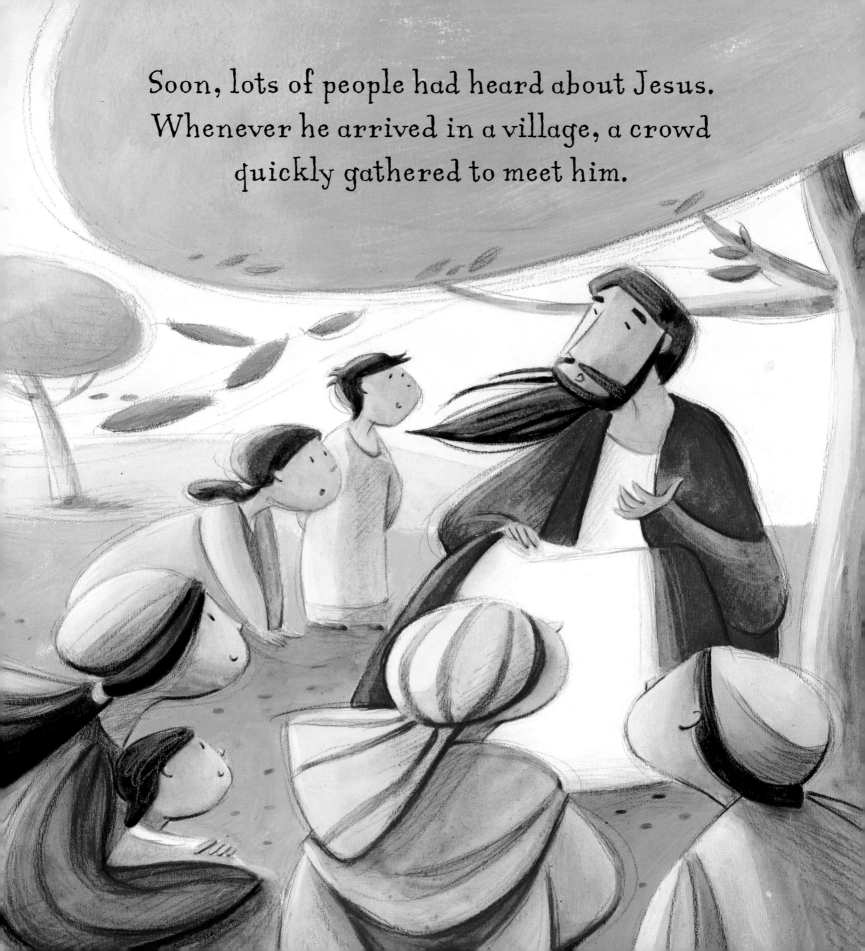

One day, a big crowd followed Jesus down to the lake. There wasn't enough room for everybody, so Jesus asked a man called Peter if he could use his boat.

Peter pushed the boat
a little way into the water.
Now everyone could see and hear Jesus.

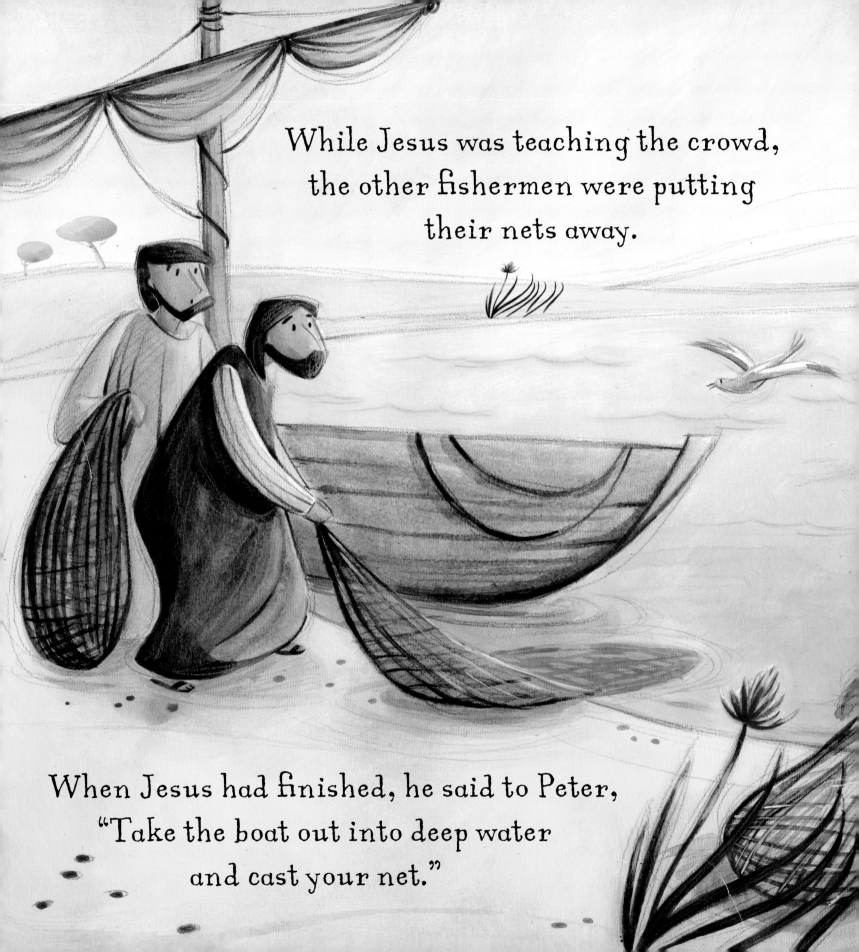

While Jesus was teaching the crowd, the other fishermen were putting their nets away.

When Jesus had finished, he said to Peter, "Take the boat out into deep water and cast your net."

"We fished all night and caught nothing," said Peter. "But if you say so."

Peter sailed to the deepest
part of the lake and
cast his net.

Soon the net was full of fish!
It was so full that the net broke.

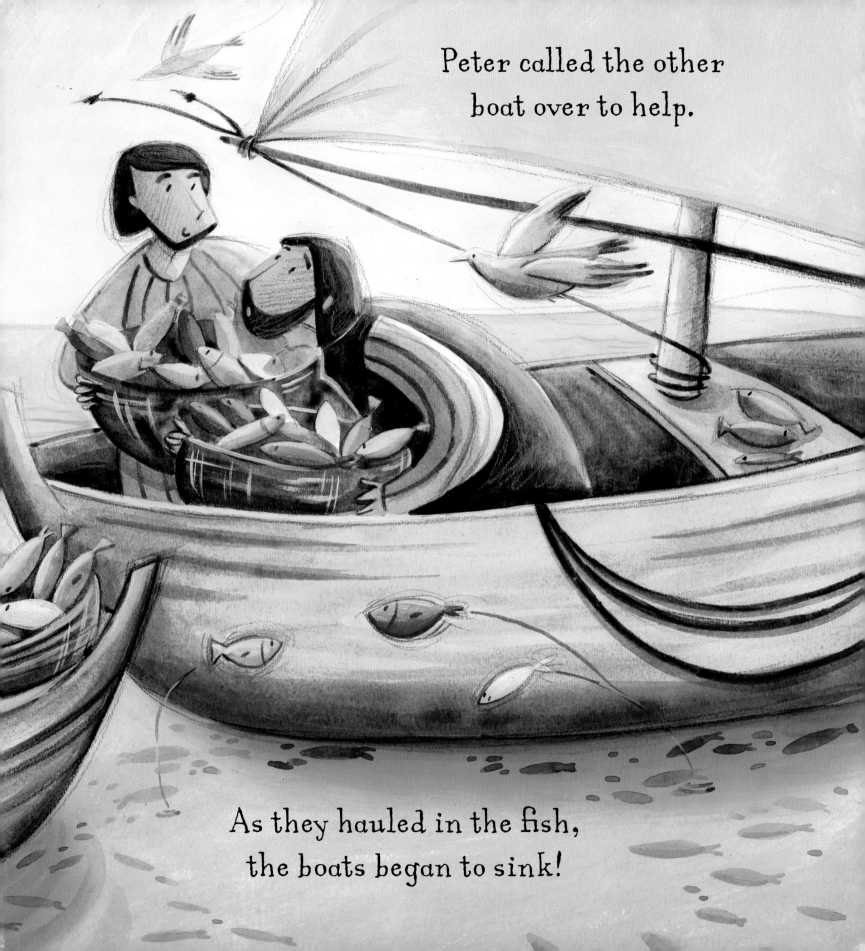

Peter called the other
boat over to help.

As they hauled in the fish,
the boats began to sink!

The fishermen couldn't believe how many fish they had caught.

FLIP!

Peter knelt down to thank Jesus, because he didn't think he deserved it. But Jesus said to them, "Follow me, then You'll be fishers of men!"

When they reached the shore, Peter and the
other fishermen, Andrew, James, and John,
left their boats to follow Jesus.

FLOP!

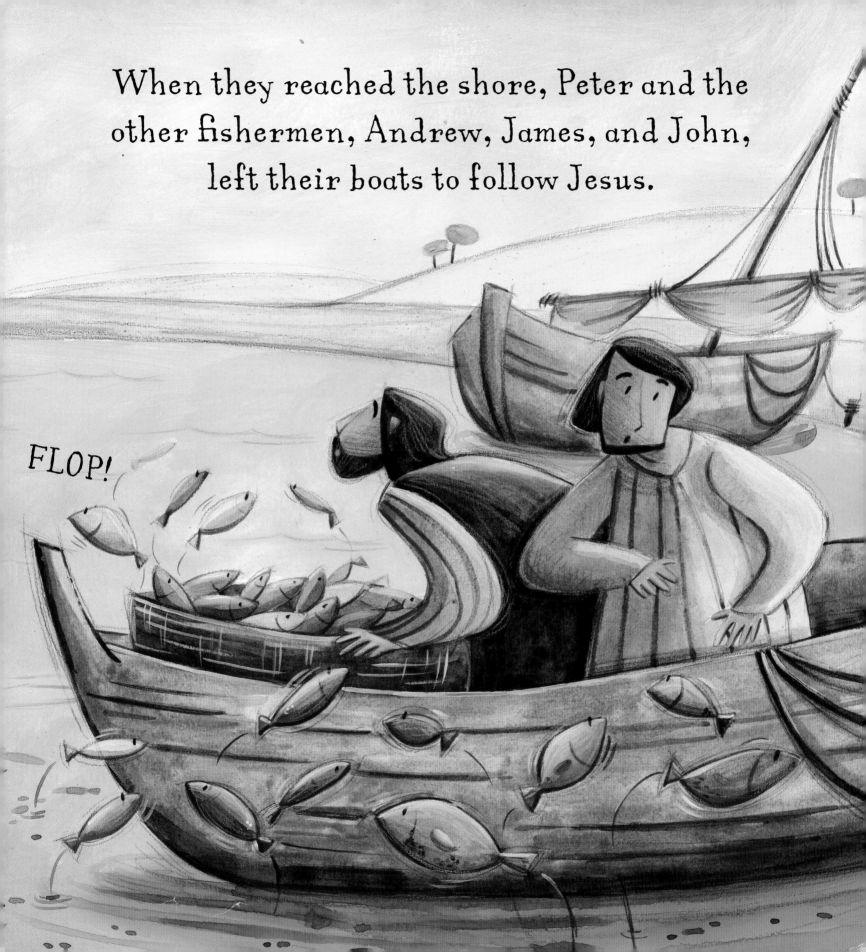

Jesus chose twelve disciples from his many followers:

Andrew,
Peter's brother

Philip

Bartholomew

Peter

James

John,
James's brother

Thomas

Matthew

James, the younger

Thaddeus

Simon

Judas

"Follow me then you'll be God's messengers," said Jesus.

One day, Jesus told a story:
"Once, a farmer sowed some seeds. Some fell on the path where birds pecked them, some fell on stony ground, and some fell in the weeds.

But some seeds fell on good soil."

CAW! CAW!

"What does the story mean?" asked the disciples.

"The seeds are the things that God tells us. Sometimes people don't want to listen to what God says, like the seeds on the path.

Sometimes people forget what God tells them, like the seeds on the stony ground.

Sometimes people are too busy to listen to God, like the seeds in the weeds.

But the people who listen to God grow stronger, like the seeds that fell on good soil."

All kinds of people came to listen to Jesus,
even bad people.

"Why do you waste time on these bad people?"
Jesus was asked. He told a story to help
everyone understand.

"Once, a shepherd was looking after a hundred sheep.
He counted them up to ninety-nine...
there was one missing.

So he made sure his flock was safe and
went to search for the one lost sheep.

"The shepherd searched and searched until he found the lost sheep.

Baa!

Baa!

He was very happy and carried it over his shoulders all the way home.

God is like the shepherd. He worries
for the bad people and is overjoyed
when they are found and sorry
for what they have done."

Next Steps

Look back through the book to find more to talk about and join in with.

* Copy the actions. Do the actions with the characters—haul up the fishing nets; scatter the seeds; search for sheep.

* Join in with the rhyme. Pause to encourage joining in with
  "Follow me, then
  You'll be fishers of men!"

* Count the disciples. Can you name all twelve of them?

* Name the colors. What colors are the fish? Look back to spot the colors on other pages.

* All shapes and sizes. Look for big, middle-sized, and small fish and birds.

* Listen to the sounds. When you see the word on the page, point and make the sound—Flip! Flop! Caw! Baa!

Now that you've read the story . . . what do you remember?

* Why did Jesus get into Peter's boat?
* What happened when Peter pulled up his fishing nets?
* How many disciples did Jesus choose?
* What happened to the seeds that fell on stony ground?
* What happened to the seeds that fell on good soil?
* Who found the lost sheep?

What does the story tell us?
Jesus chose twelve good men to help him spread
God's message.